About the Author

Dr. Marlon Paul Moseley, is a Trinidadian-American scholar and author born in LaVentille; Central Port-of-Spain, 1965. He is a writer of fiction, non-fiction, drama and poetry. This children's book is his fourth book and a remake of his very first independent short story entitled "Cream Ah De Coconut." The author developed a passion for writing at a very early age at Belmont Junior Secondary School; situated in Belmont Port-of-Spain. Once he moved to the United States in 1980, he continued his quest on becoming a prolific writer; all through George W. Wingate High School, in Brooklyn New York. Upon graduating with a Regents Diploma, he attended the renowned State University of New York; College at Oswego. It was here in 1984 that he chose his field of study in English Creative Writing Arts; and further developed a solid footing in creative writing, fiction, non-fiction, drama-playwriting and poetry. He aspires to be a natural born poet, writing prose from life experiences and of the heart. In 1989 He received his first degree; the distinguished Bachelor of Arts in English Literature & Creative Writing. He is an academic of several disciplines and holds various degrees, licenses, awards, certificates and distinction. He resides in the heart of the black community in Peckham, South London. He has lived in the United Kingdom, England; for approximately 10 years and considers himself a Londoner. He enjoys life to the full, living in his own newly built London and Quadrant flat at Burgess Park.

Dedication

I would like to dedicate the heart and soul of this short story to my elusive childhood; for which enamored me to become the man I am today. I would also dedicate this book to my mother Sylvia Jean-Jacques Moseley. She worked hard being a mother with an away husband of four children; where her parents, grandparents and ancestors settled in the former sugarcane-plantation of Belmont & LaVentille, Trinidad. Even though life was bittersweet, thank you for keeping us clothed, fed and in school. Thank you for your warm spirit and love. To my paternal grandmother Imelda Modest, whom I, my sisters and brother spent holidays with in Morvant; you were strict, but kind and fair. I remember the stories you told of growing up in the country and of my father Joseph. Thank you for being a part of my childhood. You are long gone but never forgotten and may you continue to rest in peace. And finally, to my paternal great-grandmother Maude Steele; whom I had the privilege to know, on several occasions as a boy. I always wanted to know about your history whilst as a slave girl living in Grenada. I further wanted to know what it was like for you and what those marks were on your back. I dare not ask and could not ask; as I could not even comprehend or understand your upbringing at that age. You outlived many of your children and have been in your resting place almost 40 years on. I thank you for giving me Moruga, a legacy and an ancestry. I adore the former slave quarters and Tapia House that was once your home, where your grandson my father Joseph Moseley now resides. Although his childhood was wrought with dissention in comparison to my own; he and I both understood till today, the value in descendancy and ancestry. We thank you both and will always love you. I pray that your spirit is resting peacefully and we shall meet when that time comes with warmth, admiration, love and infinity. May the power of our ancestors and God's love reign down on us always…

In Loving Memory
Of
Ms Imelda Modest - 1910 to 1978
And
Ms Maude Steele -1878 to 1981

Marlon Paul Moseley

STILL SKYLARKIN'

A CIP catalogue record for this title is available from the British Library.

ISBN 978 1 84963 820 3 (Paperback)
ISBN 978 1 84963 822 7 (Hardback)

www.austinmacauley.com

First Published (2015)
Austin Macauley Publishers Ltd.
25 Canada Square
Canary Wharf
London
E14 5LB

Printed and bound in Great Britain

Acknowledgments

I would first like to acknowledge and thank two educators whose kind words inspired me to write, and write well; when I felt my literacy being challenged. To my Scottish English teacher at Belmont Junior Secondary School in Port-of Spain Trinidad. Thank you for telling me and quote – "you may not have passed the exam, but your grade was the highest grade in the class, just stick with it and you will conquer your fear of English." To my American Creative Writing Arts professor whose name escapes me? At SUNY Oswego College. I remember you too well, you poignantly touched me on my shoulder, whilst the class critiqued my short story and you looked down at me, smiled and said, "you have something special here, this could be your niche; becoming a well-known and published Caribbean, short story writer." I was nervous to say the least. You taught the class to write not just from the heart, but from our innermost fears and happiness. You also said "writing fiction has less to do with grammaticism and more to do with expression!" Thank you both for being in my academic life, this one's for you both.

Trinidad and Tobago, which is said to be one of the richest Islands in the Caribbean because of its crude oil and other agricultural products, has yet another side, which is hardly ever seen. While most people go to Barbados or Jamaica, they seldom select Trinidad. It is not a famous tourist attraction and it can be rather expensive. All in all, Trinidad can become very addictive once it is discovered.

In the town of Port-of-Spain where the streets are often busy, there lives the Moses family. Leonard Moses, his wife Urma and their son Maxwell live in a wooden house, firmly built. They live on the poor side of town behind the East-Dry-River in a place called LaVentille. The place is very hilly and cars are sometimes found parked on the main road. Max, as he is called by his parents, goes to Catholic primary school with his friend Fredrick Williams who lives a few blocks away from him. Fred lives with his grandmother Gurdy. An old woman, in her early seventies, she took care of Fred when his mother died in childbirth. Fred was never told who his father was, but his grandmother knows he is a Yank. Fred, unlike Max, seems rather intelligent. Max, on the other hand, thinks that he is smarter than Fred.

It was a hot day on June 6th, 1973. Max could not wait until school was over and done with. His birthday was just around the corner. On June 19th he would be eight years old. Max looked older for a boy turning eight. His mother called him her little man and his father told him that he was the next man of the house.

The boys went to a uniformed school in downtown Port-of-Spain. The clothes were light brown and khaki, short-sleeve shirt and short pants, which looked rather nice. Max hated wearing uniforms, but Fred didn't mind at all. Because of the upcoming August vacation, before the school term was about to end; the teachers at their school decided to give their classes homework every other day until school finally let out. Anyway, one school day on a Wednesday afternoon, Max encouraged Fred to "Break Biche," forgetting homework and school. The boys just wanted to wet their feet in cool sea water, while drinking coconut water all day long. It was 12 noon and the school bell had just rung for lunch. Max and Fred strolled out of the school yard like it was nobody's business and headed into the heart of town.

"Max man – I doh tink dat we should do dis nah! We could get into a lot of trouble!" said Fred, as he and Max slipped out of the school gate.

"I doh believe ya! You're a year older than I am and ya acting so soft," said Max as they both made their way through a crowd downtown at the farmers' market.

"Age doh ha notin to do with dis! It's maturity and intelligence … And I tink ya is a fool for breaking beach and I'm a bigger fool for following ya."

"Where did you get all dis maturity ting from? I bet ya don't remember what year! Time! Or date! Ya born."

"What does dis have to do with anything? … Let's go home man!"

"Come on man! Just answer de question … I was born on June 19th, 1965, at 2:03am in the morning! Where were you born?" said Max, with a mighty smug look upon his face.

"I doh see dis getting us anywhere, so why not just drop it? O.K.!"

"It proves I'm a man! And I'm not scared of anything or anyone. Ya see… I always get results!" said Max, feeling confident.

"Please doh make me FART for notin! You're a man? Please!! You're only eight and I'm nine and I know when I was born, so you doh tell me what I do or don't know!" said Fred, with anger.

Max and Fred argued about their maturity for a half an hour. They made their way through the busy city to the bus station. They both ended up catching the 12:35pm bus to Chagaramus Bay! The sun started to beat down on the pavement and the tarred streets, like if the devil was doing some rejoicing. It was 98 degrees in the city and probably the whole country. Max, a tall and skinny eight-year old boy, with a lot of mouth, has just convinced his best friend to go to the beach. Fred, a nine-year old boy who still wears braids, looks over his new pair of glasses in frustration at Max. This is the first time he was ever convinced of doing something worthless. As the boys approached the bus station Max made fun of a vagrant on the street. He played a farting game as he neared the vagrant. Fred looked at him with disgust and wondered if he would ever grow up. The boys went on to talk about the heat as they waited for their bus.

"Do you tink it would ever snow and make dis place cooler Fred? Oh God man! … De sun stings so bad!"

"I heard it snowed one time in Jamaica on the mountain and it was like 65 degrees."

"Here comes the bus. You don't really believe dat do you? I think … the only place that could happen is in America."

"Do you have a ticket?"

"We'll buy it on the bus. Do you see dah vagrant on the cold concrete with the flies on his nose?"

"Why ya doh leave de poor man alone! Can't you see he needs help! He's homeless and just plain poor," said Fred, as he filled with sympathy for the vagrant.

"Come on! Move up! We doh have all day. If ya only help dah man you'll get fleas and ticks!"

Max is still mumbling about the vagrants on the street. He pulls Fred by his collar urging him to move up before he loses his spot. As the announcer made all the passengers aware of all points South at 12:35pm, the buses began to pull out. As the buses pulled out, the station had become a ghost station. The vendors were packing up and the vagrants were in their lying holes, hardly seen. The station was uniquely built and very outdoorsy. There were a few available toilets with running water; but it had that embarrassing smell of stale urine combined with Dettol disinfectant or hospital pine cleaner; it had that similar unwanted aroma of an out-house. The city and the country have developed since the sixties, when it got its independence from the British in 1962. In the seventies, there were more cars than people, making Port-of-Spain a city like all cities. Meanwhile the boys boarded the bus and were on their way to the beach. On the bus there were all different types of people, mostly of West African and East Indian descent. They seemed rather common and peasant-like. As the bus began to move the boys searched for the perfect seat. Max sat next to the back door in the middle of the bus, while Fred sat further away in the back of the bus. He sat next to an old woman with young ducklings. The woman and the ducks had a lecherous smell, which Fred didn't notice until he was comfortable. The woman was awfully fat. Her skin was much wrinkled and she covered her hair with a white hairnet. Her cheeks were puffy and when she smiled she showed no teeth.

"I ca believe I really on dis bus!" said Fred.

"Man … you mus be crazy! You doh even know where ya sitting!"

"There isn't no other seats available … what on earth is dat smell?"

"I told you dat ya better watch way ya sitting! Ya sitting next to dah woman with de shitty, smelly ducks!"

"Oh God!!! A go dead from dis smell! A smell like tootoo! I ca believe you, ya see me sitting next to de woman and ya ain't say notin! Wah kind of friend are you anyway?"

"Look, ya for eye fool! Even if I told ya where ya was sitting, ya woulda still act like a hen on eggs and sit down anyway. Look, let's move up front, our stop is next!" said Max, as they both moved to the front.

Fred looked back at the woman and he tried to figure her out. The woman looked at Fred and smiled. Her face looked like a poisonous *Puff Fish,* waiting to explode! It seemed like the woman wanted to say something to the boys, but she laughed out loud and all that showed were her gums. The bus pulled up at its stop at Chagaramus Bay and the boys ran out of the bus as though they had seen a ghost. It was rather breezy and cool. There were many Tropical Almond and coconut trees along the beach. The tide was out and the green sea moss lay flat on the rocks and sand. The boys experienced the beach as though it was their first time being there. They were looking for crabs and shrimp among the rocks. Fred, standing on a rock, saw a warship and yelled to Max, who was a bit down from him, about seeing the ship.

"Let's go out to meet the ship!" said Max.

The boys decided to take off their school clothes and leaving their jockey shorts on, they went into the water.

"You mus be mad! Look how far dah ship is. Ya cya even swim, but ya wan to go out day?"

"Don't yo no how to have any kind of fun? It's not dat far! It's just a few feet away … come on let's go!" said Max, as he swam out further.

"You could go out far if ya want, but ah swimming right here!"

"A-Rite! Forget it! Go get ya shirt and let's catch some of these fishes over here!"

"Excussame? Am I hearing you right? Why my shirt? Why not your shirt?"

"Let's just swim … I didn't come here to argue anyway."

Max and Fred forgot about catching fish and swimming out to meet the ship. Instead, they did a few handstands and a few flips in the water. They clowned around in the water for an hour. Their jockey shorts were filled with sea moss and their eyes were red from the salt water. When they decided that they had enough, the boys got out of the water and sat on the sand. As the boys looked around they saw no one, but fishermen in the distance, they knew then that they were alone and free to do as they please. Half naked, the boys let the sun dry off their brown skins as they walked along the beach and left their clothes behind. Along the bay, the boys were looking for a good coconut tree – to climb. Fred wanted to climb the first coconut tree but he could not grip the tree tight enough. Max stressed that he was taller and weighed less. Fred reluctantly gave him a boost and up the tree Max went.

"Man dis tree is so tall … Get away from the tree I'm gonna start dropping coconuts!" said Max, as he gripped tightly to the tree.

"Look wa ya doing nah! Ya almost drop a coconut on meh head!" screamed Fred, and then he started gathering the coconuts in a pile.

"Isn't dis great? Don't you wish ya could do dis?"

"I tink we have enough. Come down!"

"I'm gonna climb a little bit higher and get dat nice bunch over there!"

As Max was about to move higher up the tree, he lost his grip and fell on the pile of coconuts. Fred rushed over to help Max, thinking he was badly hurt. As he helped Max to his feet, Max groaned with pain. He was very lucky. From what could have been a bad fall, Max only received a couple of bruises and a cut over his eye.

"Max! Are you O.K.? Are you a-rite man??" said Fred, as he rushed to Max's side.

In a faint voice, Max said, "I'm O.K. I guess."

"Man … you look like a big mess. Are you sure ya a-rite? Look, I'll get some salt water to put on dat cut. Don't you move, just stay one place!"

Max sat up in pain with a cut over his left eye and what seemed to be a glowing red shiner. He was trying hard not to cry, but a tear slipped from his eye. Fred had found an old tin cup on the beach and he readily made use of it. He brought the water back and tended to Max's wounds. He tried convincing Max to go to the hospital, that they had seen a couple of miles down the main road. Max decided against it and the two boys headed down the beach and left their coconuts behind.

"W-here is meh shirt an pants?" said Max, in a horrified voice.

"I doh no!"

"I left it right on the rock over day!" Isn't dear where you left yours?"

"Nah! I left mine behind da tree right here!" said Fred, as he walked over to the tree and picked up his clothes.

"Why me man! All I wanted to do was to have some fun! Can you help me find meh shirt?"

"Sure, no problem."

"I can't go home like dis, a go catch NAMONIA AND DIE!" said Max, as he frantically searched for this clothes.

Fred and Max looked up and down the beach for the lost clothes. It seemed like they were being punished by the great sea. It was about 2:00pm and the tide was coming in rather soon. The clouds were smoky like an old brick oven, very dark and the sun wasn't shining so intensely as before. The two boys seemed very worried; Max about his clothes and both about the storm. The storm seemed rather swift and sudden. It wasn't or it didn't look like a regular passing storm.

"Here is ya shirt and dear goes ya pants!" said Fred pointing to the khaki pants as they floated out to sea.

"Dam! I'm gonna swim for dem!" said Max, as he dashed into the water.

"Forget it; they're going out too far!"

"I have to get dem or meh moda will have my hide!"

As Max swam out for his pants they kept going out further and further. He didn't care that he was in pain, he cared about the fact that he could be in more pain if he didn't retrieve only pair of school pants.

The waves started getting rough and Max could not go on anymore. As the rain began to fall heavily and the wind became rowdy, Fred picked up Max's shirt and called out for him to return.

Max had to leave his pants as a permanent loss. He knew if he had gone out more, he would have been drawn into some serious currents.

"Come on man! Forget it! There is notin you can do. Come on, the rain is fallin!"

"O.K.! I'm coming in!' said Max, in a breathless voice.

"Here is ya shirt. Put it on and let's get out of the rain. I tink a storm is coming!" said Fred, as they both sought shelter.

"What difference does it make? MAN look at me? I'm in my jockey shorts. There is sand in my shirt pockets. I LOST meh pants and above all I get to go home with a black eye!!! What am I gonna do...? What I'm GONNA DO?" said Max, in a whimpering and slightly raised frustrated voice?

Max and Fred stood underneath a broken-down shelter made out of coconut and palm branches. Fred shook and dusted his clothes and then he put them on, as wet as they were. Max picked the sand out of his shirt pockets as though they wouldn't get any more sand in them. He wore his shirt opened and he remained in his underwear until he reached the hospital. The storm disappeared like "Flash Lightning." Max wanted to comb the beach for somebody else's lost trousers and Fred wanted to get the coconut Max had picked.

"I doh want to hear another word about getting coconuts! I doh want to see them for as long as I live!"

"After all the trouble we went through, ya doh want the fruits of ya labour?"

"Look, I doh want to hear dis shit! Ya can make fun if you want! Let's just get our tails out of here before anything else happens!"

"O.K.! O.K.! Am sorry, I'm not gonna mention C.J. anymore."

"Oh! ... Ah, C.J. is what you don't want to hear about ... coconuts! And the fact that you're still in your jockey shorts!"

"Dat's really funny. HA! HA! HA! Dear is three laughs! You should go to clown school! Let's just go. The rain is easing up and it's getting late!"

"Since when are you concerned about time?"

"Not now!"

"Alright! Hey, I think you should go and check ya eye out at the hospital. It looks swollen!"

"I doh need to see a doctor, I'm just fine!"

"No you're not! If ya mother should only see ya like dis and no school pants, all HELL go break loose! It wouldn't look good atall!" said Fred, shaking his head.

"You doh worry about me, I'll take care of my own situation. Worry about dat crochety old grandmoda of yours!" replied Max, hastily.

"Ya know … ya right! What are we gonna do? How are we gonna get out of dis one?"

As the boys walk together, they are searching their minds pondering for a solution.

"Let's walk to the hospital. I have a wonderful idea all worked out and we wouldn't even get in a bit of trouble," smiled Max.

"Are you seriously thinking about going to the hospital and … getting ya eye looked at?"

"Yes!"

"Why the change and wat's dis idea all about?"

"I have decided that you, my good friend Frederick, was right about taking care of my eye. And I might be able to get some pants to wear! After all, what are friends for?"

"Oh really?"

"Yeah, really!! Dis is where my idea come into play, which I tink you would like very much!"

"What makes you tink dat I want a part of any cockamamy idea of yours?"

It was about mid-afternoon when Max and Fred took off down the main road near the seaport. There was no doubt that they were heading straight for the hospital. The boys' clothes were almost dry. As Max and Fred came upon the hospital, they ran haphazardly across the street; towards a brown concrete and brick building painted in yellow and white. The building, which was in three sections stretched out way into the back in an angular shape, which resembled a starfish. The boys entered the section in the middle and went straight to the back where the emergency room is located. Max pretended that he was in fierce pain so he would be looked at sooner. He was looked at by a tall brown-skinned man with a beard. He seemed rather young to be a doctor.

"Ouch! Dat stings man!" said Max, as he looked up at Dr. Brown.

"The way you act I swear dat you can endure a lot of pain. Just leave the bandages and the wound alone. It will heal just fine!" said Dr. Brown.

In the lobby, Fred waits and looks at the people around him. As he thinks to himself … "Look at all these people around here. I've never seen so much sick people in one place in my entire life. Dam! I wish I was home!"

While Fred waits around the emergency room, he felt scared and paranoid. He looked into some of the faces, which seemed so sad around him. One woman was constantly crying about her baby who swallowed Clorox bleach. A man had a stab wound, which he covered with a towel at his right side. Fred was trying very hard to fake a smile. Max finally showed up with hospital overalls as trousers which he got from doctor Brown and a plastic bag in his right hand where the cheeky bugger stole some bandages, gauze and iodine to incorporate as and implement as a part of his plan.

"Max! Where have you been all dis time? Come on let's get out of here!" said Fred in panic.

"What's da matter wit you? Ya know I was getting looked at by the doctor!"

"Oh, it's nothing. I just tink dat its time we get home. School is gonna be over at 3 o'clock and it's now fifteen minutes to de hour. If we don't do something soon we'll have our teachers and our parents to contend wit!"

"Where is all dis coming from? Just take it easy! Remember I said dat I had an idea?"

"Yeah!"

"Well, it's fully formulated into a prefect plan!" said Max, as he and Fred left the emergency room and headed for home.

"By da way. Where did you get does khaki pants from and what's in the bag?"

"Oh, dis? Doc gave them to me! They have lots of dem back der. He said I was a special case, seein dat I didn't have no pants atall. And I didn't even cry when he gave me foe stitches."

"You got foe stitches?"

"Yeahhhhhhhh!"

"Did it hurt?"

"NAHHH! It was a piece of cake!"

"Anyways, what's in the bag man?"

"I got bandages iodine and gauze! Dis is gonna help us get out of our situations with school and answering to our parents!"

"How is bandages gonna help us with dis here situation? Maybe if we had taken the coconuts, we could of sold dem down town and get some money for new pants for you and some apples for our teachers!" said Fred, nervously.

"Keep on dreamin. Dey're not gonna buy dat! You have to be inventive … COCONUTS! COCONUTS! Can't you tink of something else? I told you never to mention dat again!"

"Well you tell me. What are we gonna do? Tell me how dis plan gonna work? Let me hear it?"

"Remember when our teacher Mr. Bradshaw told the class dat we should learn about nature and the things in it?"

"Yeah, go on."

"Remember he said dat early man was explorers and in order to be men man must learn the way of the land ..."

"O.K. What's your point?"

"Well, dats! What we're doing and dat's what we'll say. We're finding out about nature and being adventurous at the same time!"

"I know all about adventure and all, but where does dees bandages an all come in?"

"We're Boy Scouts! Honorary of course, but it's da same principle. The bandages iodine and gauze is what we took time out to practise, by goin to the hospital so we can use to help others in trouble in the near future."

Max didn't care about the time that much; he was so thrilled that his plan would work he couldn't wait to try it out. Fred started to believe in Max's schemes. He felt somewhat confident, as Max was. As the two boys put their heads together, they strolled to the bus stop like that famous cat Morris or Chester something. They boarded the bus and began putting their plan into action.

"Boy Scouts ... I always wanted to be a Boy Scout. Dey do so much good and fun tings!" said Fred.

"Yeah … Wait a minute. I thought you didn't like any of my ideas? Wat gives??"

"Oh notin … Can't you accept a compliment? You actually sound intelligent for a change!"

"I'm glad you finally see tings my way!"

While on the bus, the boys ponder about their disappearance from school and wonders if their parents have received any word from school.

"Do you tink dat our parents know dat we're not in school Max?"

"Don't worry about it. It's not like we have phone like does other people in the big houses."

"But, they could send a letter!"

"If day do, it's not gonna get der till tomorrow anyway so…"

"But, what about when we go back to school? Wouldn't we be caned and put to stand in the corner?"

"Quit worrying. You worry too much!"

"Man. When Mr. Bradshaw sees us he'll make sure we wouldn't sit for days!"

"When Mr. Bradshaw sees us we'll just tell him what we were doing, which is using his suggestion and exploring nature!"

"Alright! Whatever you say; I am trusting you dis time!" said Fred, with a hint of doubt on his mind.

As the boys were nearing their stop, Max did some reformulating of his plans. He tried reassuring Fred that the plan was fool proof. Fred decided to go along with the plan once and for all. He knew now he had no other choice. As the bus approached the bus station, there seemed to be less and less people on the streets. The busiest part of the day was almost gone.

"Man, what happen to all does bums that was here before?" asked Max, as he and Fred stepped out of the bus.

"They went to the poor house to get food and shelter." Answered Fred.

"Man … I'm glad I'm not dirt poor. I just doh understand it. We have all dis oil money, and where is it going? To does uppidy Trini people, de man in de red house, de Yankees an dem an doh foeget dat Queen, like she ain ha enough in her bloody castle!!!" Max and Fred both giggled and laughed, about a serious subject matter and whilst upset, could see the humor in it all. They both seemed to know and care enough about their surroundings and living condition even though; they may be too young to fully comprehend the extent of Trinidadian economics.

"Trinidad is still a wonderful place. We're better than other West Indian countries." Replied Fred, with pride.

"If we're so much better off, how come we still got out-houses or shit houses as mame an dem does say? And why does da water and light go all de time? Yeah! We're better off alright!" De teacher in school say we should use the word Latrine. I guess if you say it, its sounds French and doesn't smell so bad??" Shared Max with a mischievous grin.

"Gee! Would ya stop putting de country down? I know we're not perfect, but we're still trying to make dis country a better place to live!" said Fred, being the optimist.

"If tings are getting better, how come they're vagrants and poor people beggin everywhere on the streets? I tink it's does dam Yanks, East-Indian an de people in Europe who keep buying up we land with their hoity toity selves!" Max was forever opinionated and critical for someone who had to walk to the hospital in his underwear. He felt that his plan will pull the wool over both his teachers and parent's eyes and it was indeed foolproof. What was he thinking? As he continued on Fred belted;

"Oh please! Let's jist not talk about dis anymore! We're too young to be worrying about such tings. Let de older people worry about it. We have a present matter at hand!" said Fred, as Max bumped into a vagrant.

"Watch where ya going Max!" exclaimed Fred.

"Excuse me excuse me!" says Max as he starts to calm down;

"Well, let's take our time and go over dis ting once more before we head on up the street," Fred suggested in his response.

"Alright, I guess I jist get angry when I see so many poor people lying on the streets," again mentioned Max.

"Yeah I no wat ya mean man… It does get to meh too. You sound like you actually care about those people. Is this a change of heart towards dem?" asked a concerned Fred.

"It's nottin, let's go!" said Max, as they both neared Independence Square.

Independence Square is where most of the traffic is situated. Taxis and pedestrians are both busy. The Lord Cipriani statue is situated in the central park, where the pigeons usually land. You can see the flight of the "Scarlet Ibis" and also hear the sound of the common bird the "Cobow," or Vulture as it's known; which is a scavenger bird that congregate near a dumpsite called the Labass that gives Port-Of-Spain a mephitic smell. There are many sub-tropical plants, flowers like the hibiscus and balisier flower neatly displayed and planted in the heart of the square. There are also many Almond, palm and coconut trees situated all along the square. The temperature has just dropped to an even 88 degrees as the boys make their way up LaVentille.

"Well … anyway. What's the plan again?" said Fred, wanting to be sure.

"For de last time, dis is wat ya do… First when ya get home you will show your grandmoda de bandages an gauze. Explain to her what you learned and what inspired you. You will tell her dat you were jist following what Mr. Bradshaw said, which is exploring nature and helping others. Tell her dat you're an honorary Boy Scout and you learned how to make First Aid bandages. She would love to hear dat! Dat's wat all parents want their sons to be, nice respectable young men!" said Max, in a very proud tone. But a young liar nevertheless and encouraging Fred to do the same.

"What if she asks meh why meh clothes is so dirty? And what if she received the notice from our teachers?"

"Jis stick to what we planned. And emphasize what Mr. Bradshaw said!"

"O.K.! Den wat about school tomorrow?"

"Like I said, stick to de original plan and we'll have Mr. Bradshaw and everybody eating right out of the palm of our hands!"

"Let's go to it den!"

Max and Fred were only a few blocks away from their homes. Max followed Fred home to see how his plan went into action. As Fred approached his home he could see his grandmother sitting on a bench on the front porch. The house was made out of oak, cedar and brick with galvanized roofing very common to this day. Mrs. Gurdy, or Grumpy Gurdy as she is called by all, is sipping black coffee from a wooden cup. She is constantly looking over her bifocals and into the street. As she walked towards the front of the porch in her green moth-eaten duster, she thinks she sees what could be her grandson and calls out to him.

"Freddy!! Is dat you dear boy?" said Mrs. Gurdy, in a hoarse voice.

"Yes Grandma!" said Fred, as Max follows him in and ducks down behind a rose bush.

"Boy! Where have you been all dis time?" inquired Fred's grandmother.

"Ah…Well…ah, school over a little… well… actually, me and Max was doing something dat Mr. Bradshaw wanted us to do!"

"Attaboy Freddy, dat's de ticket!" said Max, to himself thinking out but quietly.

"What! I can't hear ya, get up closer and stop mumbling, speak up!" said Mrs. Gurdy.

As Fred talked on, his grandmother got more annoyed. She grabbed Fred by his shirt collar and shoved a letter in his face. She asked him questions about his whereabouts, but he could not answer. Max, seeing this, tried to sneak away, but his shirt was caught in a branch of her prickly cactus plant.

"Well! Well! What is dis all about? SPEAK UP YOUNG MAN!"

"Well ma ya see."

"You're gonna get it dis time! No more sparing de rod to spoil de child!" said Mrs. Gurdy, as she pulled out a 2-by-4 from behind de bench. It looked like a ruler, but it was much thicker.

"Holy shit everything tun olemas!" said Max, as he was stunned to see the size of the thing.

"Grandma! Please doh beat meh Nah. Leh me explain," said Fred, as he was almost in tears begging his granny to be lenient.

"Damn! I am getting outta here!"

As Max took off Fred got the whipping like you would not believe. While on the way home, Max could only think that what was once a brilliant plan just went up in smoke. He went on believing that his plan would work. He blamed Fred for not being strong enough and not sticking to his marvellous storyline. He started thinking out loud as he reached his home. As he entered his front gate, his mother Urma was on the stairs and she seemed very happy to see him. His father Leonard, on the other hand, looked at Max with an impish smile.

"Ah! Mame! Daddy! Dad, what ya doing home so early? You're probably wondering wat happen to me? Let me explain why I got dis bandage on and …" As Max was about to explain, he was interrupted by his mother with his father looking on and smiling patiently waiting for Max to dig himself out of the hole he has fallen into long ago.

"Oh! I already know what you were up to!" said Mrs. Moses, with a smile on her face.

"It's not what you tink. I was being a Boy Scout!"

"Go wash up for dinner," said Mrs. Moses, in a somewhat indignant tone.

"A-rite Ma, I'll be right back!" said Max, as he headed outside towards the sink.

"Dat boy! Will he ever learn? Who does he tink we are? Look at dis letter!" said Mrs. Moses, as she showed her husband the letter.

"I know jist what de boy needs… some time away in the country, up in Toco with his grandmoda Willie. She'll work him to the bone! And ya know she doh make joke!" said Mr. Moses.

"I'm all washed up ma. What are we having for dinner?" As he rushed back into the kitchen, petrified about what will happen to him.

"Your favourite! Crab and CALALOU, with the cream of de coconut, giving it dat stewed taste! Also I have sweet potato pie, coconut cream pie, for desert and coconut water with de jelly in it! Come on and eat up, I've been working all day on all dees dishes just for you!" said Mrs. Moses, as she set the table.

As Max began to eat dinner, he felt disgusted. He did not feel like eating food. As it was rather ironic that his parents did not give him a thrashing like Fred's and the last thing he ever wanted to see, taste, eat or smell was anything with coconuts.

"Dis taste good hon!" said Mr. Moses.

"Ya better stop playing around and eat ya dinner. Thanks hon! I doh no wat's wrong wit dat boy today nah! I didn't make dis food for it to go to waste!" said Mrs. Moses in a calculating manner.

Max immediately gulped down his food for fear of his behind.

"I'll eat!" he said with a mouth full of food.

"Don't speak with ya mouth full! Don't tink, I doh no ya wasn't in school today, but we'll spare you dis time," said Mrs. Moses, regretfully.

Max had a sign of relief. He felt he had gotten away by the skin of his teeth. He only had to contend with school and Fred the next day. He felt rather lucky.

"I'm gonna do my homework now."

"Yeah ya better finish all of ya homework and bring it for me to check!" said a happy Mrs. Moses. As she and her husband was about to exact the sweetest punishment on their dear son.

"Oh …ah son by the way, after school let out, how would you like to spend some time in the country with your grandmother Willie? She hasn't seen you since you were a baby!" said Mr. Moses with all smiles.

"Oh, sure ting Dad. The beach is near, right?"

"Yeah! Oh and prepare to be helpful. She needs a big strong man to help her prune and pick her coconut tree!"

"Say WAAAAA!"

Trinbagonians Colloquial Meaning: Parts of speech, dialect and vocabulary

A

ah-yah-yai: an expression of anticipation or pain, etc.

A lime; to lime; liming: To hang around with friends and acquaintances, indulging in "ol' talk" and giving "fatigue", enjoying drinks and delicacies perhaps, for an indefinite period of time at a given location.

allyuh: all of you people

A fete: to fete; feting: Not to be confused with an informal "lime", a fete is a full-blown party with copious amounts of food and drink. The more crowded the fete, the better. Music and dancing are essential elements.

ax: ask, to ask a question

B

bacchanal: rowdy, scandalous behaviour; good party, minding another's business and adding to, thereby causing confusion

back back: suggestive dance, the male dancer's front rubbing against the female's rear and vice versa

bad eye: a look of anger or reproach, especially when looking from the corner of the eye

badjohn: a bully, a dangerous man, a gangster, someone with a reputation for hurting people

Baigo: Tobago

bam-se lambay: attractive female buttocks

bam bam: backside, behind, arse, bottom, buttock

bobolee: a person who is habitually taken advantage of

bol-face: bold face, pushy, loud and wrong, unreasonable, demanding

boo-boo -lups: fat, clumsy ungainly person

boof: to insult, castigate, yell at or argue with

buh wait nah: but wait a minute, now hold on

buljol: a dish of shredded saltfish with onions and tomatoes, avocado, pepper and olive oil

Break Biche: School children cutting classes, getting into mischievousness', fun and trouble without care or consequences.

C

callaloo: soup or stew of African origin made from dasheen leaves with okra, boiled with pumpkin, coconut, salt meat or crab

calypso: a musical and lyrical comment on any subject, profusely composed for, but not limited to the Carnival season

calypsonian: a singer of calypsos like Shadow Winston Bailey who was raised in the village of Les Coteaux

channa: Indian word for chick-peas or split peas

cheups: a derogatory sound noise made by sucking your teeth, also indicates a negative or no response, probably origin is the Congo where it is still part of speech

chupid: stupid, foolish

coki-eye: cross-eyed

commesse: confusion, controversy associated with argument, gossip and slander

Congo Betsy Congo Brown Congo Ellis: supernatural being from African witchcraft and myth

cut-eye: a look of anger or reproach, especially when looking from the corner of the eye

cyaa, cyah: can't, can not.

D

dasheen: leaves that are finely chopped with a special wooden 'dollie' which has ochroes added, boiled with pumpkin, coconut, salt meat or crab to make callaloo soup or stew that is of African origin made from

dingolay: to dance with joyful abandon, to flaunt, to tease playfully

doh, dough: don't, do not

dong: down

doo doo, doux doux: sweetheart often used with darling, as in dodo dahling - the French doux means 'sweet'

doogla, dougla: a person of mixed race, usually African and East India

dotish, doughtish: stupid, foolish and dumb - probably from the English doltish

dress rong: move over, shift, I need a seat

drevait, dree vay: wayward person, to knock about

E

eh eh: an exclamation of surprise or indignation, often said with much emphasis for effect - Eh - What did you say? Eh eh - No, no way, oh no. Eh heh - Oh really? I understand. Yes

enless: plenty, endless.

ent: isn't it, is that not so, thats true

F

faddah: fada: father

fall out: to stop speaking with someone or to terminate a friendship

fete, fet: a party, loud music, lots to eat and drink, dancing to wee hours of the morning

flim: film, a movie

founkie, foong-key: foul smelling, stink odour

free up: relax, let go

fresh-water yankee: a person who spends a short time in the USA and returns with a heavy American **accent;** originally, one who acquired a 'yankee' accent by simply visiting a US military base or the US Embassy

G

Gang Gang Sara: an African witch involved in legend where the mermaids came to play

go-bar: nonsense, foolishness

goinorf: someone who appears to be going out of their mind, acting strangely

gun talk: fighting words, to threaten verbally

gyul: gyal: girl

H

hair: here or hear

harden: disobedient

hops: crisp bread roll, often filled with ham

horn: to cheat on a spouse or lover

horner man: a guy who makes love to someone's wife

huggish: rude, crude, mean; the behavior of a thug or gangster

hut: hut meh: hurt, to hurt someone

I

in ting: in big people ting: to be involved in current activity. Or young people being nosey about adult conversation.

is so?: is that so?

J

jabjab: a carnival clown-like devil character

jadoo: 'magic' used by a woman to charm a man

jamet: a 'sweetman' or kept lover

jamette: a prostitute

jook: jook-jook: to stab or punch at anything, a sudden forward hip motion

jouvert j'ouvert: British authorities decreed in 1843 that the festivities could not begin until Monday morning. Since no time was specified, the carnival goers began to celebrate on the stroke of midnight - the origin of the wild procession known as j'ouvert that begins Carnival today and culminates with the sound of steel bands, the participants covering themselves with mud and then proceeding to splatter all the bystanders with it - all in good fun.

jumbie: (v) to harass, to annoy ,to irritate

jumbie: (n) traditional characters or demons that can either be mild or very malignant

jus now: in a little while

K

kalenda: stickfighting which is thought to have originated in the use of bamboo sticks to fight fires in the cane fields

ketch: catch

Klim: a generic word for any brand of powdered milk

koskel: weird, strange

L

La Diablesse - la-ja-bles - 'Female Devil,' or 'She-Devil': She is a very pretty woman who wears pretty dresses with full petticoats. Late at night she lures men to her with her beauty. These men are usually coming home from the bars and are drunk. However, what the men don't know is that she has one good foot that she normally shows and one cloven calve's hoof that she hides. She lures men to cliffs where they can fall to their death.

langniappe, lang yap: a little extra, a bonus

las lap: last lap, last minute street partying on Carnival Tuesday just before the official end of Carnival at midnight

lef: left

lef dat: leave that

leh we: let go

leh go: foul smelling, stink odour

lick dong yo: hit someone or something, to topple over

licks: a beating, a physical punishment

like ting: to be somewhat mischievous

limbo: a funeral song and dance of African origin is performed each night of the week following a funeral, accompanied by hand clapping or stamping of bamboo sticks (tamboo-bamboo).

lime / liming: (v) hanging out, having fun, as 'Let's go down to the corner and lime.'

liming: (n) a wildcard word for any social event like cinema lime, pub lime, party lime

locho: a loafer, a lazy person, a parasite

M

maco: someone who minds other people's business to gossip

macommère: a female companion or friend

macocious, makocious: one who is prying, nosy

magga: very thin, skinny

makaforshet: left-overs; from the French 'ma ca fourchette' - 'food stuck between the fork'

make style: show off, tantalise

maljo, maljoe: bad eye, or evil eye

malkadee: blight, unhealthy, ill

mamaguy: trying to fool someone, or being fooled by someone, to falsely praise, eg. Your friend is wearing an ugly dress, but you tell her that it's beautiful

mamapoule: hen-pecked husband; a derogatory term for a husband who seems to be controlled by his wife, a weakling, easily taken advantage of

mama yo: expression denoting shock and surprise

mas: masquerade, carnival

matter fix: everything is well organized, everything is OK

mauby, maubi: bark of the carob tree colubrina reclinata used to make a drink of the same name

moko jumbies: stilt dancers, an African tradition carried over into carnival - their costumes represent jumbies, or beings from the dead

mooma: mother

mouter: a boaster - to much mouth

mo vey lang: bad tongue, slanderous

much up: to pamper, to butter up

mud band: a j'ouvert mas band with revellers plastering their bodies in mud from head to toe

N

nah: no - negative

nanny: vagina

nastiness: an expression of disgust applied to a good-for-nothing person

neem: a culinary spice from a 'sacred' tree - used in some form on a daily basis - the twigs as a toothbrush, the oil for soap, and the leaves for medicine. Veppam, margosa. Azadirachta indica

ning ning: tired eyes

now fuh now: instantly, right now

no wherian: person of no fixed abode

O

obeah: traditional characters, practices and belief

ochro: okra or lady fingers

obzokee: awkward, out of place, misshapen

ogun: a god of a faith of African origin that takes significance from the elements and the force of nature

okra: lady fingers, vendakkai, benakaayilu

ol' talk: empty chatter, nonsense, eg. 'What you're saying is a bunch of ol' talk.'

old hag: traditional characters

one han cyaa clap: one hand can't clap - a bribe will grease the wheels, be good to me I'll take care of you

one set ah: a lot of anything, plentiful

own way: stubborn person.

orisha: a faith of west African origin that takes significance from the elements and the force of nature

P

panyard: where steel bands reheass

Papa Bois: - bwa - translated from French-Patois 'Father of the Woods'. He is responsible for the lives of all of the animals in the forests and it is said that when hunters get too greedy, he takes revenge on them - either by damaging their guns so that they can no longer hunt or so they injure themselves, or by making the hunters get lost in the forests and other such stunts.

parang parran: people that sing at Christmas time about the birth of Christ in their parang songs. Parang is derived from the Venezuelan-Spanish word 'paranda' which means to go from house to house to fete. The colloquial term for 'parran' is the abbreviation

pastelles: seasoned mincemeat mixed with olives, capers and raisins in a cornmeal casing and wrapped in banana leaves; a culinary legacy of the Spanish settlement, traditionally served at Christmas

pelau: rice dish with peas and meat and flavoured with coconut and pepper - from India

pholouri: fritters made with split peas

pissin tail: a person of no class or importance

planasse: to hit someone with the flat side of a cutlass

Q

qualey: withered, dried up

qua-qua: a percussion instrument which, with hand-clapping often accompanies 'bongo' music.

querk: an irritating person

R

raff: to grab suddenly, to take away something from someone

ragadang: broken down, derelict

ram cram: packed to capacity

roti: a thinly cooked dough which is filled with a curry mixture which can contain beef, chicken, goat, shrimp, any meat or potatoes - from India

rude: nasty, sexually explicit

S

saga boy: a male or female who is boastful of his physical attributes, flashy dresser, dandy

sampat: an unfair attack, ambush

scizzors: poom-poom - vagina.

screw pan: an angry or determined look on a person's face; usually makes them look humorously ugly

shadow beni: a herb known an cilantro used for its distinctive seasoning flavour, added to cooking meats giving a distinctive taste

shif yuh / carcass: move yah ass: move over, get going.

shub, shove: move or cast aside.

skin up / yuh nose: turn up ones nose

skinnin yuh teet: grinning

Skylarkin: to idle, waste time

sometimeish: moody

Soucoyant / sucuyant - soo-koo-yah: she is an old woman who lives by herself in an old rickety house. Late at night she peels off her skin, turning into a ball of fire that flies over the entire island. She stops intermittently and sucks the blood from sleeping individuals. She has to return to her home before sunrise or else she will die. She can also die, if, while out of her house, salt is sprinkled on her skin. When she returns to her skin she will shrivel up and die. It is believed that you can protect yourself by sprinkling salt around your bed before retiring for the night.

The way you can tell if you've been bitten by a soucouyant is if you awaken and you're bruised. This is how some account for waking up with black and blue marks - which could have occurred the night before or even the day before and to account for why old people tend to stay home a lot.

T

tabanca: the feeling of hurt when a romantic relationship ends

tantie tante: from the French for Aunt

tamboo: variable lengths of bamboo knocked down to make a drum-like sound.

tarmbrin: tambourine

teef: thief

tent: Kaiso tent - a venue - a calypso or soca concert featuring several singers, music bands and comedians

tick: thick - overweight

tight: intoxicated, drunk, and stoned

ting: thing

toolum: one of the earliest candies from the slave days, made with molasses and grated coconut

toti, toto: male genitalia, penis

tot tots: female breasts

U - V

umpteen: plenty of anything, often

vampin: pomin stink: farting - producing anoffensive smell.

vaps: suddenly behave excitedly or strangely

vex: vexed, angry

vikiey vi: evasive, unreliable, and indecisive.

W

wais: rong yah wais: waist I.e to hold some around their waistline.

wajang: rowdy, uncouth person

well yes: expression of disbelief.

wha happenin dey?: what's happening?

wha'ppen?: what's the matter with you? - How are things?

when cock geh teet: it will never happen

whey: where

whey yuh say?: what did you say?

wine winin: sexually suggestive dance using rhythmic hip gyrations

wrong-side: the worst pieces of bad luck is for a fishermen is to go fishing with his clothes put on inside out.

Y - Z

yampee: mucus found in the corner of the eyes after sleep

yemanjah: a god of a faith of west African origin that takes significance from the elements and the force of nature

yuh faddah head: expression indicating disgust

yuh look fuh dat: it's your own fault

yuh makin joke: you can't be serious

zaboca: avocado

zug up: de man   zug up meh head: Uneven haircut. An uneven cutting